- The Fairies -
Petal & Nettle
and the
Big Birthday Surprise

For my family.
Thank you for always believing in me.

Kirstie x

Telltale Tots Ltd.
www.telltaletots.co.uk

First published in the United Kingdom by Telltale Tots Publishing 2021

ISBN: 978-1-9162549-8-5

A CIP catalogue record for this book is available from the British Library.

Text and illustrations copyright © Kirstie Watson 2021

- The Fairies -
Petal & Nettle
and the
Big Birthday Surprise

WRITTEN BY

Kirstie Watson

ILLUSTRATED BY

Tilia Rand-Bell

One day, Petal and Nettle were playing a game…
"I spy with my little eye, something
beginning with… F," said Petal.

Nettle looked around. "Forest?" he asked.

"NO," said Petal.

"Hmmm. Feather?"

"NO," said Petal, "do you want a clue?"

But before Nettle could answer, Petal swished her
wand, and all the flowers began to bloom.
"Flowers," he sighed. "Petal, it's no fun if
you keep using magic - it's CHEATING."

"Okay, no magic this time, I promise. I spy with my little eye, something beginning with B," said Petal.

Nettle didn't even have time to think before an excited Petal blurted it out...

"BIRTHDAY! It's your birthday tomorrow! And I'm going to get you the BEST, most special birthday gift ever!"

"Oh, Petal, that's lovely, but remember the most special gifts are thoughtful - not ones just conjured by magic," Nettle teased.

This gave Petal the most wonderful idea...

...She would arrange a magic-free, surprise birthday PARTY for Nettle. It would be very 'thoughtful', and she'd prove to Nettle that she COULD do things without magic.

She rushed off to start planning.

Firstly, she needed some party decorations. But she didn't know ANYTHING about making decorations by hand.
She was just beginning to wish she'd learned when something COLOURFUL caught her eye...

"FLOWERS!" she cried,

spotting a beautiful garland. Nettle loved flowers.

It was utterly perfect, so she took it.

"Now I need a birthday CAKE. But what do I know about baking?" she fretted, just as a wonderful aroma wafted, unexpectedly, under her nose.

She followed the delicious scent to the most

scrumptious looking cake she'd ever seen.

It was perfect, so she took it.

Next, she needed to find the perfect PRESENT.

But she didn't know the first thing

about present-buying because magic

could always whip up the perfect gift.

But just then, she heard the most delightful

JINGLING, TINKLING sound.

Petal followed the sound to an exquisitely beautiful BELL.
It was simply hanging there, JINGLING and TINKLING all alone.
It would make the PERFECT gift, so she took it without another thought.

On her way home, Petal found
a few more things...

...some snacks and drinks...

...fluffy cushions for the
guests to sit on...

...balloons...

...and a music player.

"Perfect. Now I have almost EVERYTHING
I need, and I did it all by myself!"
Petal said proudly.

"All that's left is to invite our FRIENDS."

Off she went to deliver the invitations - by HAND.

But as she dropped off the last one, she had a little NIGGLE.

"Hmmm. Have I forgotten something?" she wondered.

But, if she had, she couldn't think what it could POSSIBLY be, so she put the worry out of her mind.

The next day, as Petal was busy preparing for the party, there was a sudden knock at the door. RAT-A-TAT-TAT!

"Oh no! They're early!" she muttered, opening the door to...

...some VERY unhappy friends.

"Whatever is the matter?" Petal asked.

The fairies explained that a sneaky thief had

taken their special birthday gifts for Nettle.

"That's terrible! WHO would do such a thing?" Petal asked.

"Errr, I think it was YOU!" said one fairy, pointing at the bell, garland, cake, snacks, drinks, fluffy cushions, balloons, and music player.

"ME!? But I just found these things... I didn't think they belonged to anyone... I just didn't know how to do it all by myself," she said sadly.

Then Petal realised what she'd done. She'd taken these things when they actually belonged to others. She hadn't even asked, and that was very WRONG.

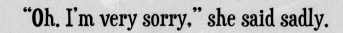

"Oh. I'm very sorry," she said sadly.

"Thank you for apologising," said one friend.

"But, if you needed help, you should have asked us," said another.

"Well, I could use some help now," Petal suggested.

The fairies didn't hesitate to lend a hand.

Under Petal's instruction, they worked
TOGETHER to create the best birthday party ever.

Once everything was ready, they waited patiently for Nettle to arrive.

They waited...

...and waited...

...then Petal suddenly realised what she'd forgotten.

"Oh no! Nettle! I forgot to invite NETTLE!"

"That's ME!" said Nettle, appearing at the door.

"Wait! Is this a... PARTY?"

"SURPRISE!" everyone shouted quickly.

"Wow. Everything looks FAN-MAGICAL-TASTIC!
This is the best surprise EVER! You must have used magic for this!?"

"No, actually, I planned it all by myself... without magic,
BUT I did have some help from my FRIENDS," Petal confessed.

"I just forgot that one small thing... to invite YOU!"
Nettle giggled. They all giggled. Then they laughed and LAUGHED
until they couldn't laugh anymore.

Petal had discovered that she was EXCELLENT

at party planning – even without using magic.

She was PROUD of herself for trying her best,
and knew that if she ever needed help
she could always ask her FRIENDS.

But she was, of course, delighted to have her wand back...
to help with the tidying up.

Thank you for buying my book!

I hope you've enjoyed meeting Petal & Nettle.

Reader reviews are like MAGIC for an author like me.

They help bring attention to the book, and help

others decide if they'd like to buy it too.

So, if you like this book, please consider...

1. Telling your FRIENDS.

2. Telling ME! I'd love to hear from you.

Send me a message via: kirstiewatsonauthor.co.uk

3. Leaving a REVIEW on Amazon or Goodreads.

Kirstie x

Grab your free activity pack:

kirstiewatsonauthor.co.uk/resources

Follow me:

f facebook.com/kirstiewatsonauthor

O instagram.com/kirstie_watson_author